W9-AKX-938

Start-Off StorieS

COUNTRY MOUSE
and
CITY MOUSE

By Patricia and Fredrick McKissack

Illustrated by Anne Sikorski

Prepared under the direction of Robert Hillerich, Ph.D.

CHILDRENS PRESS ®

CHICAGO

Library of Congress Cataloging in Publication Data
McKissack, Pat, 1944-
    Country mouse and city mouse.

    (Start-off stories)
    Summary: An easy-to-read retelling of the well-known fable
about two mice and the discovery they make.
    [1. Fables. 2. Mice—fiction] I. McKissack, Fredrick.
II. Title. III. Series.
PZ8.2.M45Co   1985   398.2'45293233 [E]   85-12759
ISBN 0-516-02362-4

I am a Country Mouse.
This is my country house.
It is not big. It is not new.

3

But I like my house.
Here is why.

One day a City Mouse
came to my house.
I did what I could
to make him happy.

But the City Mouse
could not be made happy.

My house was not new.
My house was not big.

"I do not like what you
have to eat," said the
City Mouse.

"It is good for me,"
I said.

City Mouse told me about his house.

"My house is big. My house is new.

9

It is fun, fun, fun,"
he said.

"I like it here," I said.
City Mouse said, "Come
to my house. We will eat.
We will have fun."

So I went with City Mouse.

His house was big.
His house was new.

13

I ate. I had fun.

Then one day, I heard
something.
Wham! Bam!

Then I saw something.
It was a truck.

Then a man came.
Then another and another.
Bam! Wham! Slam!

"Help, help," I said.

"SH-hh-hh-hh," said City
Mouse. "They will go away
soon."

"When?" I asked.

At last the men went away.

"Come out, Country Mouse," said City Mouse. "Now we can play."

But I could not play.
I could not eat.

The city was not fun.
I was not happy.

So I came home.

City Mouse can have his
big house.

City Mouse can have his
new house.

My house is old, but it
is my house.
My house is little, but
I like it.

I eat what I find, but
I am happy.

WORD LIST

a	came	go	is	now	this
about	can	good	it	old	to
am	city	had	last	one	told
and	come	happy	like	out	truck
another	could	have	little	play	was
asked	country	he	made	said	we
at	day	heard	make	saw	went
ate	did	help	man	slam	wham
away	do	here	me	so	what
bam	eat	him	men	something	when
be	find	his	mouse	soon	why
big	for	home	my	the	will
but	fun	house	new	then	with
		I	not	they	you

The vocabulary of *Country Mouse and City Mouse* correlates with the following word lists: Dolch 77%, Hillerich 85%, Durr 80%.

About the Authors

Patricia and Fredrick McKissack are freelance writers, editors, and teachers of writing. They are the owners of All-Writing Services, located in Clayton, Missouri. Since 1975, the McKissacks have published numerous magazine articles and stories for juvenile and adult readers. They also have conducted educational and editorial workshops throughout the country. The McKissacks and their three teenage sons live in a large remodeled inner-city home in St. Louis.

About the Artist

Anne Sikorski is a free-lance illustrator and designer in Chicago. She has written and illustrated many books. Anne also enjoys print making and designing giftware.